Miffy's Adventures
Big and Small

Miffy Rides a Bike

Based on the work of **Dick Bruna**
Story written by **Maggie Testa**

Ready-to-Read

Simon Spotlight
New York London Toronto Sydney New Delhi

SIMON SPOTLIGHT
An imprint of Simon & Schuster Children's Publishing Division
1230 Avenue of the Americas, New York, New York 10020
This Simon Spotlight edition May 2017
Published in 2017 by Simon & Schuster, Inc. Publication licensed by Mercis Publishing bv, Amsterdam.
Stories and images are based on the work of Dick Bruna.

Manufactured in the United States of America 0317 LAK
10 9 8 7 6 5 4 3 2 1
ISBN 978-1-4814-9563-9 (hc)
ISBN 978-1-4814-9562-2 (pbk)
ISBN 978-1-4814-9564-6 (eBook)

Miffy has a new bike!

Miffy rides her bike.

Snuffy chases her.

Snuffy barks at the ducks.
The ducks quack back.

Snuffy and Miffy race.

Snuffy is in the lead.

"Going up hills is hard,"
says Miffy.

“Going down is easy!” says Miffy.

She goes too fast.

Miffy falls.
She hurts her ear.
It is good that she is
wearing her helmet.

Miffy and Snuffy go home.

Miffy tells her mom
about her fall.

Her mom knows
how to help.
She gives Miffy a
bandage.

Miffy does not
want to ride again.

“When you fall,
it is best to get
back on,” says her dad.

Miffy puts on her helmet.

She will try again.

At first she feels afraid.

But soon she feels better.
This time
she rides slower.

Snuffy runs ahead.
Miffy rides slowly
after her.

Snuffy is hurt.

Miffy knows how to help.

“Follow me,” says Miffy.

Here is a bandage
for Snuffy!

Miffy puts on
the bandage.

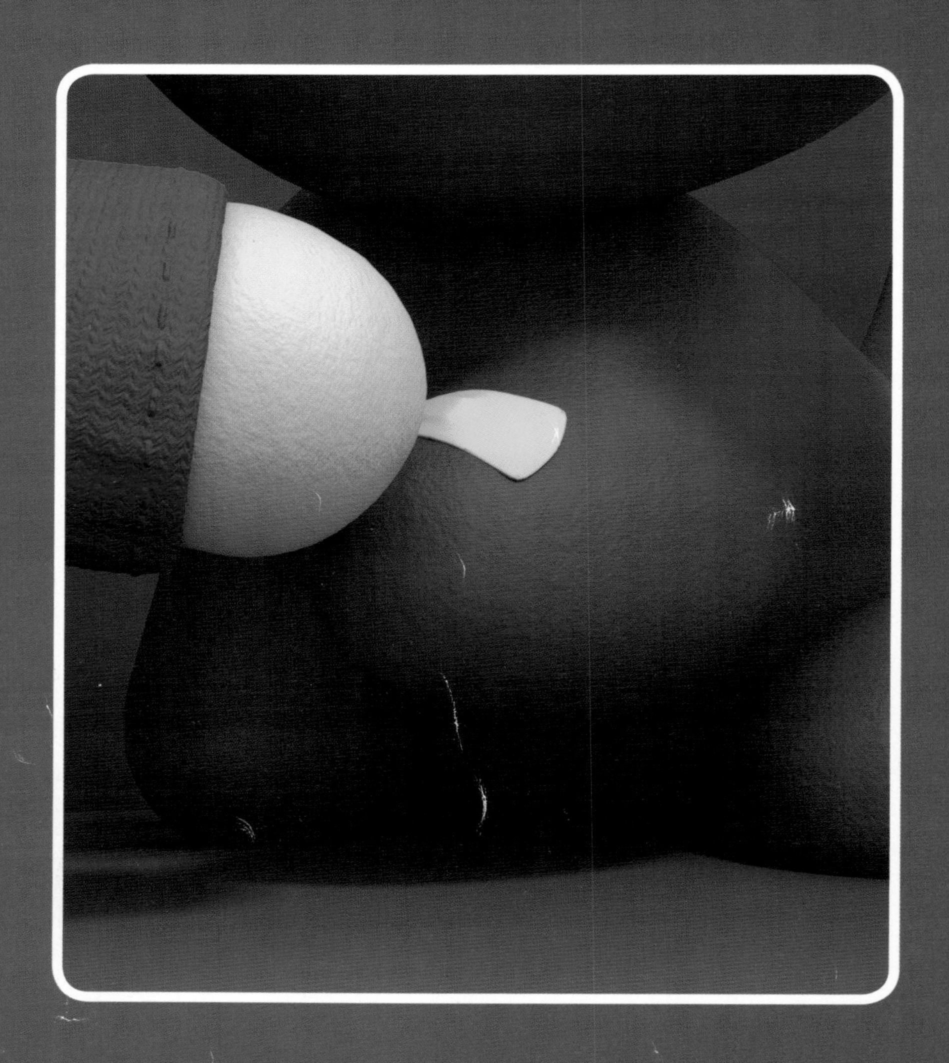

Miffy and Snuffy match!

Now it is time for

a little cake.

Then Miffy rides again!